בס"ד
לד' הארץ ומלואה

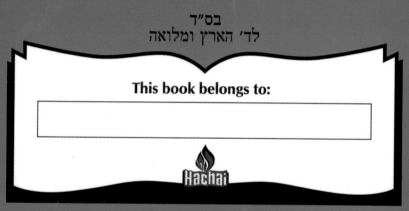

This book belongs to:

Please read it to me!

I Go to
the Doctor

written and illustrated by
Rikki Benenfeld

Hachai
PUBLISHING

Special Thanks to Dr. L. and all the caring
Doctors and staff at Pediatric Associates.

In Honor of Moshe and Devory B.,
Special brother and sister-in-law. R.B.

I Go to the Doctor

First Edition - Tevet 5764 / January 2004
Second Impression - Nissan 5766 / April 2006
Third Impression - Adar 5769 / March 2009
Fourth Impression - Tishrei 5771 / September 2010
Fifth Impression – Adar 5773 / February 2013

Editor: Devorah Leah Rosenfeld
Managing Editor: Yossi Leverton
Layout: Eli Chaikin

ISBN-13: 978-1-929628-15-5
ISBN-10: 1-929628-15-3
LCCN: 2003112075

HACHAI PUBLISHING
Brooklyn, New York
Tel 718-633-0100 Fax 718-633-0103
www.hachai.com – info@hachai.com

Special thanks to Eli Rosen, M.D.
Jeffery Teitelbaum, M.D.
and Rita Sachs, R.P.A.,
for reviewing the material included in this book.

Printed in China

I Go to the Doctor

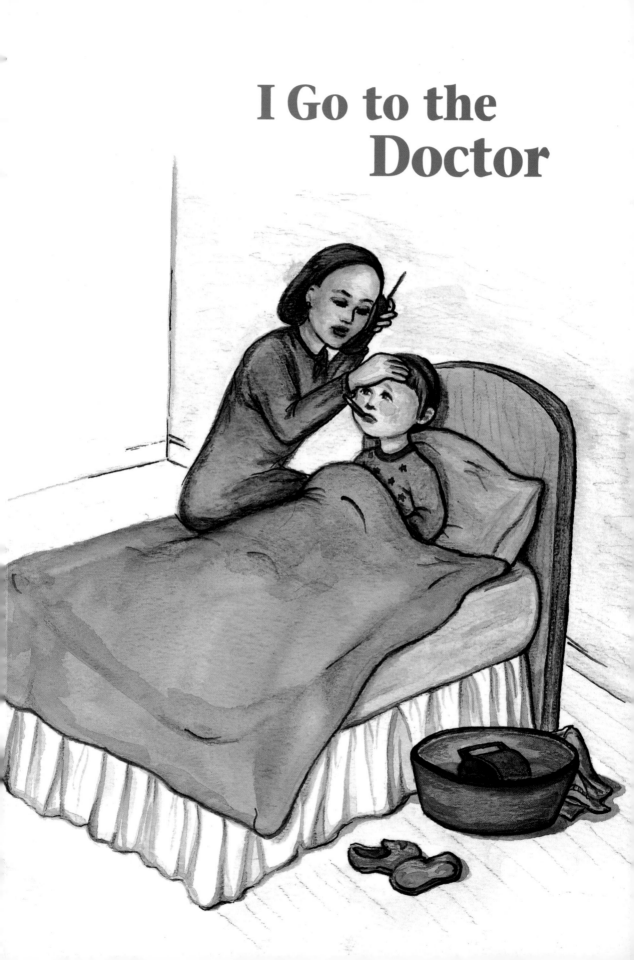

I'm going to the doctor,
My mother's taking me.

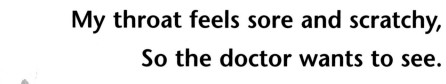

My throat feels sore and scratchy,
So the doctor wants to see.

The waiting room is busy,

It's full of girls and boys.

Until it is my turn,

I read a book and play with toys.

The nurse comes out and calls my name,
We follow her right in.

She says, "Take off your shoes now,
We're ready to begin!"

I step up on the big, white scale,
The nurse checks how
I've grown.

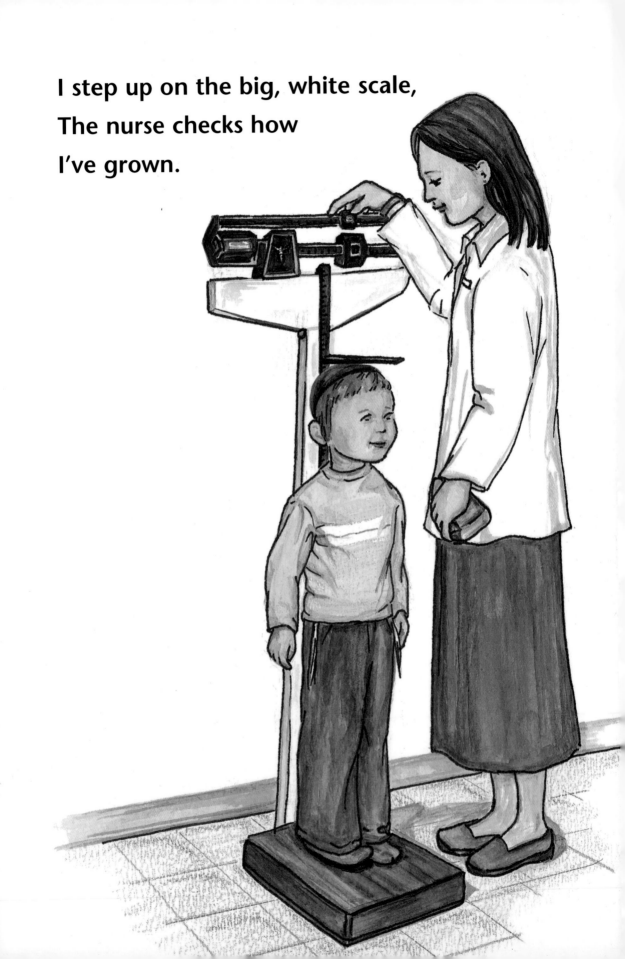

There's paper on the table,
And I jump up on my own.

Then she takes my temperature
To check how hot I am.

"The doctor's coming in," she says,
"And he'll do your exam."

The doctor smiles
    and says, "Hello,"
He's wearing
    a white coat.
I know Hashem
    will help him
To fix my poor
    sore throat.

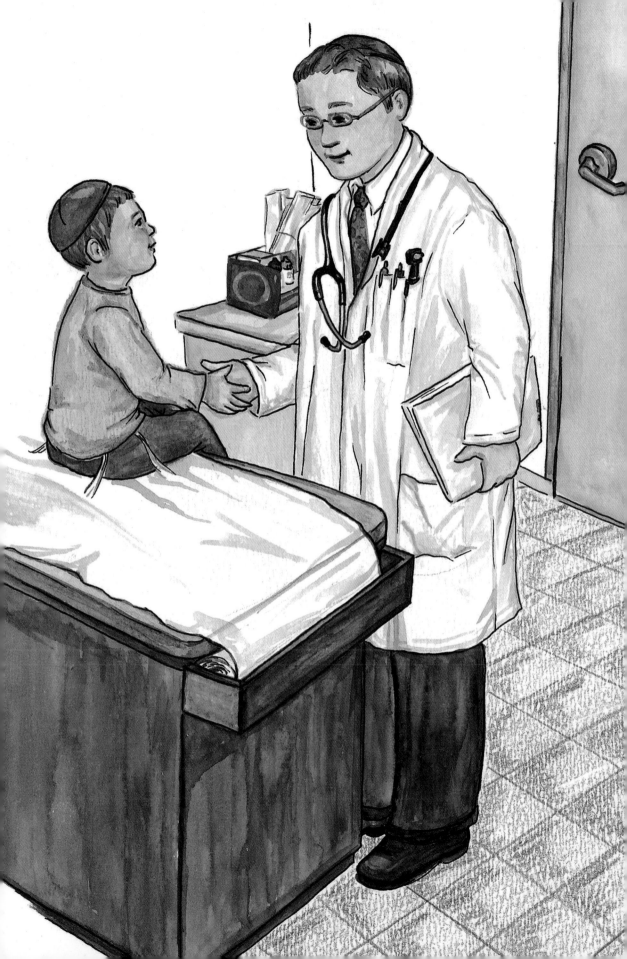

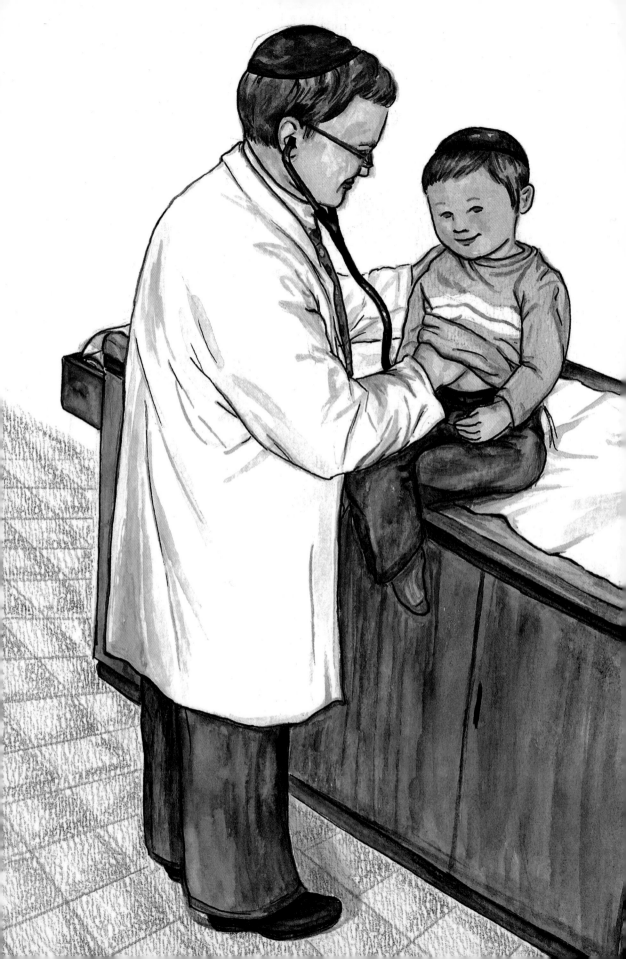

The doctor holds a stethoscope
That's cold against my skin.

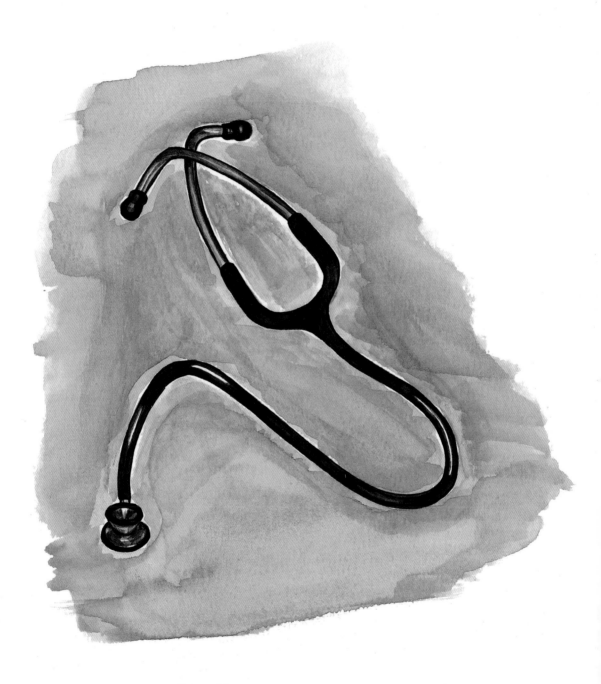

He listens to my heart and lungs
As I breathe out and in.

With a pointy otoscope
He looks into my ear.

Then he checks the other one
And says, "They both look clear!"

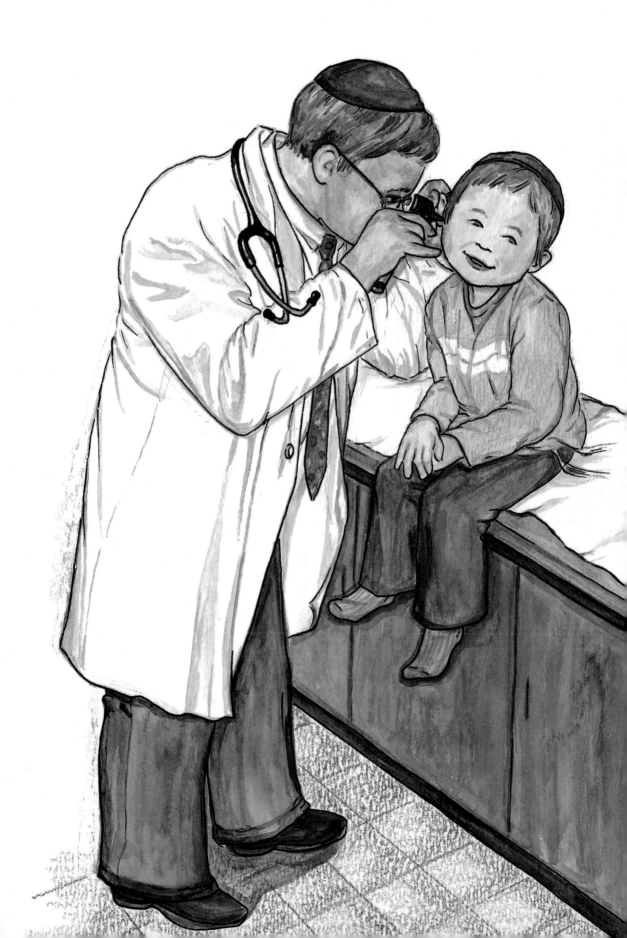

The doctor shines his little light
And tells me, "Open wide."

I say, "Aaah," stick out my tongue,
And let him look inside.

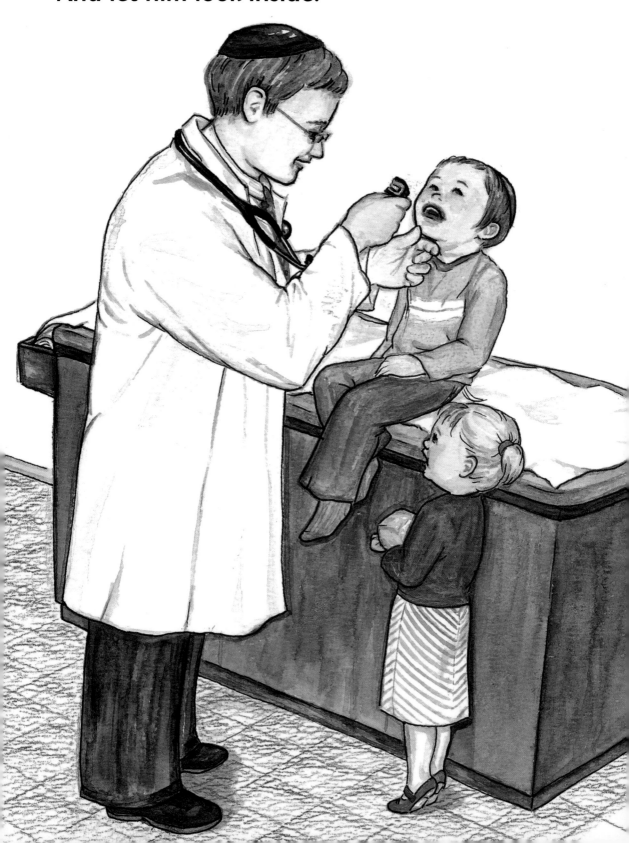

The doctor says, "Your throat is red,
I'll put this swab down in it."

I don't like the way that feels,
But it just takes a minute.

He says, "You'll need some medicine,
One spoon, three times a day.

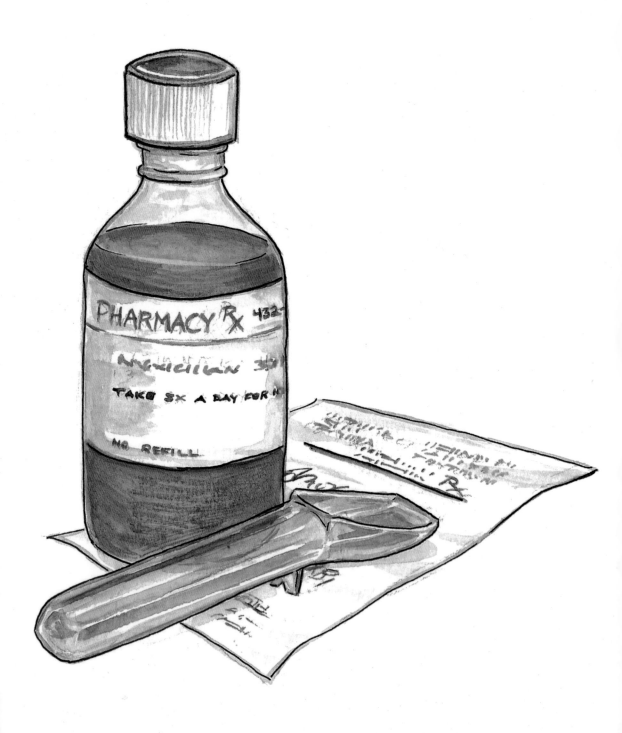

And very soon, your poor sore throat
Should start to feel okay."

The doctor gives me stickers,
And I stick them on my sweater.

Then he asks me, "Do you know
Who really makes you better?"

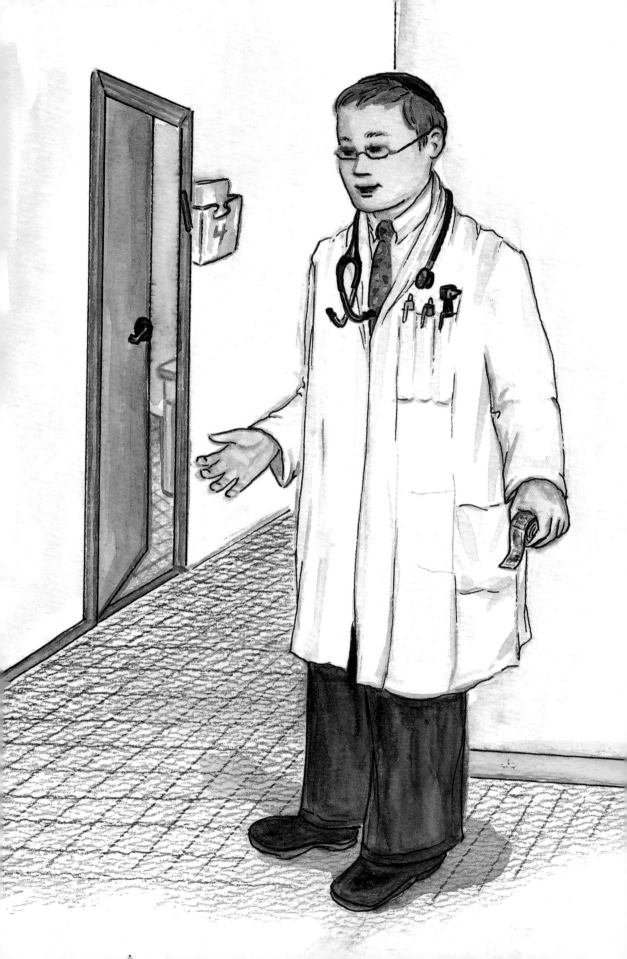

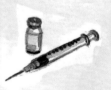

"Hashem helps doctors,
nurses, too
So they can take
good care of you.
Take your medicine,
and then –
Hashem will make you
well again!"

"Thank you, Doctor. Thank you, Nurse."
I wave goodbye to them.

And, of course, I give
The biggest 'thank you' to Hashem!